Dedicated to my favorite thieves—Michael, Max, and Dagny—who stole my heart.
—Vijaya Bodach

Reycraft Books
55 Fifth Avenue
New York, NY 10003
Reycraftbooks.com

Reycraft Books is a trade imprint and trademark of Newmark Learning, LLC.

Library of Congress Control Number: 2020908276

ISBN: 978-1-4788-6813-2

Printed in Dongguan, China. 8557 0620 17230
10 9 8 7 6 5 4 3 2 1

Author photo courtesy of Vijaya Bodach
Illustrator photo courtesy of Nayantara Surendranath

First Edition Hardcover published by Reycraft Books

Reycraft Books and Newmark Learning, LLC, support diversity and the First Amendment, and celebrate the right to read.

REYCRAFT
BOOKS

To Ivanna,
the Chota Chor
of my heart
—Nayantara
Surendranath

LITTLE THIEF!
CHOTA CHOR!

WRITTEN BY
VIJAYA BODACH

ILLUSTRATED BY
NAYANTARA SURENDRANATH

Astrange chattering woke Anjali. She rubbed her eyes. "Mama!" she whispered, but Mama rolled over, sound asleep.

The clock ticked.

Tap-tap-tap. The night watchman's stick broke the stillness.

Anjali climbed over Mama and lifted
the mosquito net just enough to slide her
legs out. Her feet touched the floor. It felt
cooler than usual, and when she looked
toward the door…it was wide open.

Anjali shook Mama.

"WAKE UP! THERE'S A THIEF!"

But Mama stayed asleep.

"Maybe we forgot to latch the door shut," Anjali said to her doll.

Anjali tiptoed across the cold floor and closed the door. She struck a match and lit a diya. The oil and cotton wick in the small bowl caught fire quickly. As the shadows rose, Anjali shivered.

Scrambling into the kitchen, she saw that the jars of pickles, chutneys, and jams stood silently on the shelves.

Burlap sacks containing flour, lentils, and rice were tied closed.

Pots in a corner nestled one inside the other. Not a thing was out of order. Even the fresh fruit basket remained untouched.

"The thief wasn't hungry," Anjali said, breathing easier now. But her mouth was dry. She dipped a cup into the large earthenware pot filled with water and took long gulps.

"Now let's see if anything was stolen," Anjali said, walking to the front room. Her eyes had adjusted to the dim light of the diya. The two beds joined together took up more than half the space.

Books, clothes, sheets, and sundry items were
still stacked neatly on the built-in shelves. But...

"My sparkly skirt. It's gone!" It was her prettiest. Mama had sewn in tiny mirror daisies.

"What else did you take, thief?" Anjali ran her fingers along the desk. She stroked Mama's velvet purse, soft as moss growing on tree bark. She snapped the purse shut, then clicked it open again. The coins were gone. So was Mama's silver comb— her only treasure.

"Mama! A thief was here." Anjali clutched
her doll, opened the front door, and
shouted at the top of her voice,

"THIEF!
CHOR!"

The night watchman and the neighbors quickly gathered outside. Mama rushed out as Anjali told them everything—how they'd gone shopping, and now the missing things. The neighbors all talked at once.

"POOR CHILD!"

"MONEY STOLEN!"

"WHO WOULD DO SUCH A THING?"

What a racket! Everyone searched the street for the thief, but Anjali scooted back inside.

"Why take my pretty skirt? Why not food?"
Anjali whispered to her doll.
"Maybe the thief has
a little girl."

That's when Anjali noticed that her tin box underneath the desk was also missing. She laughed as she imagined the thief opening the heavy box in a dark alley, hoping to find gems.

"The thief—he stole my box of river rocks?" Anjali scratched her head. Why would someone want her smooth and pretty rocks? "What if the thief is a little girl?"

Anjali clasped her doll.

"We must find her! If she has no family, she can be my sister. Oh, she must be frightened. She would hide and I know just the place."

Anjali ran outside, behind the house,
to the peepal tree. Her favorite hideout.

Something twinkled in the dark. Her skirt!
As Anjali went toward it, a few stones fell
around her. Her stones.

Anjali looked up—
a little monkey bared
his teeth. A flash of silver.
He held Mama's comb.

The monkey grasped the comb to his chest, chattering and clambering higher.

"I see that you don't want to give it up," said Anjali. "Maybe..." She ran back inside and returned with a bunch of bananas.

She peeled one and started to eat it slowly. "Come, little thief, chota chor!"

A shower of stones rained down along with the tin box. The neighbors gasped. The monkey chattered some more.

Anjali peeled another banana. She held it out.

The monkey scrambled down—
closer. Anjali smacked her lips,
making kissing sounds. The monkey
copied her. He held out the comb.

"For you, chota chor!"

The exchange occurred in an instant.
Mama, the night watchman, and
the neighbors clapped!

"I could tame him," Anjali said.

"Tomorrow," said Mama, gathering Anjali's skirt and tin box. "We need to get some sleep. What a night!"

Anjali cuddled up to Mama.

Her woodsmoke smell made Anjali feel safe, along with the faint *tap-tap-tap* of the night watchman's stick outside.

And Anjali slipped into sweet dreams
of her Chota Chor and their many
adventures to come.